Brian Orca
a fable in novella form

by Bill Hoffman

Adult/Child
Literary Fiction

"Whenever you find yourself on the side of the majority, it is time to pause and reflect."

Mark Twain

Acknowledgement

As a child, when awake, I shuddered badly. But in my dreams, I flew to unknown places so gorgeous and unique that speech was superfluous.

Thank you, Dr. Yagalucci. You taught me mind quieting and cured my stuttering.

However, traveling by dream was lost to me when the stuttering disappeared--an equitable sacrifice. Still, I miss falling out of bed right after a wild trip amongst the clouds.

CHAPTER 1
Porpoising

It was late morning, and the sun was high. The air was still. Bright sunlight glinted from series after series of smooth, rounded swells. Brian Orca dipped under the calm water, angled his head slightly upward, kept his pectoral fins true, and flicked his tail. His flukes responded with a quick whoosh. He shot forward, gliding on the surface like his much smaller cousins often did, reaching a speed no whale or shark could sustain. He repeated the sequence, increasing his pace until he felt like he was flying through the water. He was playing—his belly was full, and he was celebrating his achievement of a special kill.

The bull walrus he gutted was the first big mammal kill he had seconded. He killed as his father held the big bull by the head. Brian Orca ripped its entrails from its body in a crushing bite. First blood tasted so good, so fresh. It was special. It was wonderful.

His family feasted on the rich liver and oily blubber as Brian Orca redoubled his effort, trying to porpoise faster than he ever had. He skimmed the water, gliding on it for a moment, slicing through it just under the waves, hydroplaning on the surface, then back to slicing the water.

He wasn't the only one celebrating. His mother and father were just behind him. Both were longer and more powerful than he was and terrific swimmers and 'porpoisers.'

They caught up to him.

His father glanced at his mother. "Now is the right time," he said.

"Praise to Wassemo," his mother answered.

"Did you see me?" Brian Orca asked. "I did it! I'm ready to lead a hunt!"

"Of course I saw you. I was there!" his father said.

"I know! You held him well!" Brian Orca twirled once in the water. "I did it! I got us a walrus!"

"You did," his mother said.

His father glanced at her. Brian Orca thought he looked thankful—probably because she was putting the lesson back on track.

"Why do you insist on sliding like that? Like this," she said. She used her peduncle and caudal peduncle muscles to sharpen the angle of her tail and snap her flukes. She was graceful and powerful, but he was already almost as fast. "Wassemo taught our ancestors this exact movement," she said. "You should execute it precisely." She whipped her flukes quickly downward, upward, downward again, and upward with great force.

From the tone of her clicks, he knew she was showing him her technique despite a bit of frustration. She was not only correcting him for the umpteenth time, but she was showing off. She was showing off her power as much as her technique.

"But I like to porpoise like this." He flicked his tail as hard as possible but with less angle than his mother, causing a burst of speed, and he instantly followed up with slower but wider-angled flicks. His motion looked slower and less abrupt but kept his body straighter, and he found he could maintain a full porpoise for a while.

They raced; his mother had some water on him as she was a quarter body length in the lead.

"Stubborn boy!" she said. She ticked shrill and fast in odd, serious laughter. She was having fun, despite herself, he thought.

He whipped his tail faster, and, in a moment, he was even to her. His mother's lesson was not lost on him.

She angled her head upward, whipped her tail, and shot out of the water. Her entire body was airborne. A full breach. She fell back, and water sprayed and jetted out from under her. Brian Orca felt, heard, and saw the concussive force of her power.

Brian Orca looked back at his mother as she was surfacing. He thought he could beat her in a short race, maybe not a long one. He wondered if she had breached to distract from the fact that he had managed to porpoise faster than her for a moment. He was not yet an adult, and he matched her. It was a guess, assumptive, and others would say cynical. Still, there was perhaps truth to it. And even at his age, the truth was important to him.

When he looked forward, he angled his head to join her and saw a massive shape before him. His father. He cut Brian Orca off. Brian Orca flicked his pectoral fins to slow down and angled his flukes. He barely adjusted in time to avoid colliding with his father.

"Boy!" said his father.

Father did that on purpose! Brian Orca thought as he shot by him. "Really," shrieked Brian Orca.

"He never listens!" she said. "Never!"

"Awareness!" his father said. Brian Orca wasn't sure if his father was addressing him or his mother.

"Mother goaded me!" Brian Orca had already figured out he had blown it as he stopped. He knew this lesson wasn't about speed or even proper technique. Anger welled in him. He wasn't going to stick around for another lecture. He was celebrating—*come on!* He had been having so much fun. He was tired of his parents' never-ending criticism.

"Did she now?" his father said.

Brian Orca porpoised again. His parents immediately followed suit, and the three found themselves in unison of motion, familial unison of movement.

Such rare unison, especially within a family unit, was a point of pride, and Brian Orca was instantly happy. They had fallen into a oneness that his pod cherished. He knew his parents were thrilled.

"What *is* your lesson today?" asked his mother.

She ruined the moment! He thought. "I don't know. How about that? I don't know. I'm stupid!"

"Stupidity is not your problem." His mother was frustrated and sounded a little hurt.

The three of them slowed to swim, which immediately turned chaotic, each taking the lead and losing it to the one who, at the moment, was the most perturbed.

"How about not trying to better yourself in a race because Father will just interfere," Brian Orca said. His clicks and high whistles were full of sarcasm. His parents were too controlling, especially when they were together and focused on him. When they were together, they were like barracuda, he thought. *They are obsessive and mean.* His dorsal was growing out, and they were still lecturing him!

"I'm a teenager. I'm almost an adult," he said. "You should treat me like an adult."

"Silly boy," said his mother. "He already told you the lesson, but you don't listen."

She broke the surface to take a breath and was quickly back. "Difficult one," she added.

"No, he did not! And you didn't listen to me." Brian Orca watched his father for a reaction while arguing with his mother. He was not hopeful of getting anywhere with his mother if his father agreed.

His father, the pod's eldest male and most powerful orca, shot under them and disappeared into the depths. Brian Orca immediately turned his attention on his mother to show he purposely ignored his father showing off. He hid that he was concerned his father might have left angry. Both his parents had tempers. All orcas are moody.

"You don't know?" said his mother.

"He didn't even give me a clue! And you won't! You never do when he's in surprise lesson mode."

"Son, you have years of learning yet. Wassemo spelled out our lessons long ago, which has done our community well. They keep us fed, and they keep us safe. Our kind has prospered because their Songs of Ages, their original lessons, are the truth. Wassemo teaches us life is many lessons."

"Seems like one big lesson."

"Really?" his mother said with unveiled sarcasm.

Wassemo, now we're getting into a fight, thought Brian Orca. Well, that was better than listening to them about the almighty and all-wise Wassemo. The four-in-one who died for all orcas. They—Wassemo—wanted perfection and would return to enforce their ideal, or so it was promised.

"Wassemo, forgive me," he said. "You wouldn't want to ruin one of Dad's surprises by giving me a hint. Why make me guess all the—"

Brian Orca's father cut him off, purposefully glancing against Brian Orca's side as his father shot by him and burst out of the water, committed to a complete, vertical breach. His father shot straight up. He came crashing down, underside first, causing a massive splash.

His father recovered quickly, and before Brian Orca reacted, his father was snout to snout with him. "Well?" his father said.

"Well? Well, what!"

"Brian Orca," his father said. "You do not use all your senses all the time. Are you orca? I don't understand you! Awareness, son! Awareness of your surroundings! You didn't even sense me approaching."

"That's not fair!"

"Sure, it is," his mother said. "Have you ever been able to surprise us? No."

"The world is full of danger, son. Rogue sharks. The apes. Giant squid."

Brian Orca was surprised to hear his father, one of the mightiest bulls, say such a thing. His father wasn't afraid of anything except Brian Orca's grandmother and his mother when she was angry.

"The pod protects you," his mother said. "Wassemo protects you."

"And our family protects you. We can protect you because we always know our surroundings. We know what's around us. But you don't know what's around you. Even your little sister is more aware than you. Awareness allows you to consider options, choose the best, and act. We have no equal because we live cooperatively, and we all know what's in front of us, under us, above us, and behind us."

Brian Orca hardly heard his father. He was still furious at the Little Miss Perfect insertion into their conversation. He looked out toward where he thought the rest of the family was. He had been frustrated, but bringing his little sister into this was too much!

He focused on what he had just heard. He clicked rapidly in protest, loud and high pitched; several pod members answered back, a couple imitating him in rapid clicks and squeals. They were listening to the argument, and the two had taken it upon themselves to mock him. They were laughing at him!

"With that attitude, you will never survive a day alone!" his mother interrupted. She was serious and angry.

Brian Orca turned slightly, curved his fins, and whipped his tail as hard and fast as possible to escape his parents. He was just below the surface and wasn't swimming toward anything, just away. It was unfair his mother goaded him into ignoring his surroundings, so his father had an excuse to lecture him about it. "Enough. I'm gone. And I won't come back," he said to no one and everyone.

"What kind of son leaves his pod? It's not done. What kind of son leaves his mother?"

He sped up. He would show them. He would leave the pod for a day—no, two days! He would show them he could survive… even thrive on his own. He would return after they were worried sick that he might be dead!

He swam off at a burst and slowed down to a fast swim. He swam near the surface and was beginning to get into a steady, fast, sustainable pace. His mind clouded in anger and judgment when a big orca cut him off.

Again! he thought, believing the orca to be his father. He banked and angled upward and broke the surface. It was a clumsy maneuver.

"What an idiot!" he raged. *My father is insane for cutting me off*, he thought.

He stopped just above the big orca and looked down to see it didn't have the long dorsal fin of his father. The orca was his grandmother.

"High One! I'm—I'm sorry! I didn't see you!"

The pod's matriarch did not move. "Come here."

Not good, Brian Orca thought. He descended in a half circle to comply and stopped in front and slightly below her, showing her proper deference.

"Oh please," she said with a bit of irritation.

He ascended to her level. "I… You surprised me."

He wanted nothing more than to approach her and nuzzle her. She had always been his relief from his parents. But he knew if he did, he'd stay.

"Where do you think you're going?" she said flatly.

"Away!" he whistled. "Away!" he added in loud and rapid clicks.

"Attitude, Brian Orca." She opened her mouth wide and moved her head from side to side, telling him in their clan way to calm down.

Brian Orca noticed something odd about her mouth. A piece of something grayish on her teeth and under her tongue. He looked closer. She had seaweed in her mouth.

"Grandmother?"

She quickly closed her mouth. Brian Orca sensed she was embarrassed.

"Oh, I didn't quite get it all down. Terrible-tasting stuff." She chomped and swallowed. "It helps the stomach." She added, "It helps an old orca restore herself."

Seaweed. His grandmother *was* getting old. *She's our knowledge giver, and she eats seaweed.*

"I'm not kidding. It heals."

"I'm leaving, and I'm not going to let you stop me," he blurted out.

"I have no intention of trying to stop you."

"But you just did. Stop me, I mean."

"Only to ask where it is you think you're going?"

"Away." He wanted to be angry. But until now, he hadn't considered he was leaving her, the one who was always kind and was always there when life was tough. And what about the rest of his pod? And the clan? He was leaving them as well.

But he'd be back. This was only to teach his parents a lesson.

"Away can be a short distance or a very long distance. Or a distance in between," his grandmother said.

Maybe it's not such a good idea to leave, he thought. He hadn't thought it out at all. Her presence was poking at his soft spot, tugging at his decision.

"Follow Wassemo's ways. You have free will, and they will not be pleased if you rejoin the Great Blue before your time."

Despite bringing up Wassemo again, he immediately realized she was, in her way, telling him to be careful, and not to die, and that the pod wouldn't be happy if he did die.

He expected her to back off a little, permitting him to leave, but she did not. Brian Orca hesitated. Did he want to go? Was she testing him? There would be ramifications when he came back. But he had to show them, even his grandmother, who seemed to give him a mixed message.

"You aren't ready to test yourself."

"I think I am, and I'm not testing myself."

"One never knows. Go back to your parents."

"No."

"Excuse me?"

"No."

"You're not ready."

"I can hunt."

"I'm not talking about hunting or even awareness."

Brian Orca tried to go around her, but she maneuvered in front of him again.

"Tell me you swim with Wassemo. Tell me you believe as we do. They will watch over you."

Brian Orca averted his eyes and, silently but respectively, inched forward.

"Please," she said.

He wished his family would stop evoking Wassemo all the time. All the important lessons he had learned were said to be passed down the generations and were credited to long-dead porpoises who had never spoken to him to date. He had never felt their presence. His parents didn't even seem to think for themselves sometimes, and when they did, when they tried something new, if there was a hint of success, they always gave credit to them. His grandmother could be no better, he realized. After all, she had passed down the ways to the pod; she was why the old ways endured.

"Come back alive," she implored.

Brian Orca wanted to avoid promising anything. And if he said he would be back soon, it would impact the lesson he wanted to teach his parents.

He passed her in silence, which was very difficult for him to do.

CHAPTER 2
Tail Lobbing

He had no idea where he was going, just away from the pod. After significantly longer than he had ever dashed in a mad porpoise, he slowed down but swam faster than usual. He'd show his parents and his grandmother. *They won't find me when they come looking!*

Hours passed, and night finally came. He continued to swim, and when it came time for him to take a long resting break, he discovered a loneliness he never thought existed. For his entire life, his pod took resting breaks throughout the day and night between meals, socializing, and traveling. They would go into a sleep pattern for up to six or seven hours. They would swim together slowly and in a tight group, even synchronizing their breathing.

Now, he was alone and could not be as one with his family.

It was a tough night, full of self-imposed abandonment, and it gave him a chance to consider turning around and rejoining his pod. He rested for three hours, then continued the rest of the night.

When the sun rose, he was in the partially enclosed waters of a large fjord, and he had not lost his determination to teach his parents a well-deserved lesson.

After many more hours of constant swimming, only breaking the surface for air, he saw a massive shoal of herring. The shoal was just in front of him and to his left, and hunger struck at the sight of the multitude of little fish. He hadn't eaten for a long time. *How could you not know the herring were in front of you before you saw with your eyes?* He imagined his parents chiding him. He sent out a high-pitched echo to tell the others of the fantastic find, and for a moment, he was ecstatic because he was the one who found them. More proof he was an adult!

But of course, there was no answer. *Oh right, my family isn't here.*

He swam into action, diving under the fish. He circled under them, trying to herd them into a tighter mass.

Try as he might, the fish avoided balling up because they could avoid him better by not clumping together. One inexperienced orca was not enough to terrify thousands of little fish.

Still, Brian Orca was not one to give up quickly, and he keyed in on a specific fish, snapped his flukes to give chase, and caught it and another in quick succession. But he knew he expended more energy catching the tasty but small fish than what he would get out of them.

The chase had taken him away from the shoal, and he was suddenly tired.

Brian Orca wasn't sure what to do. Chasing a bunch of little fish by himself wasn't working, and now he knew firsthand why his pod went after a shoal as a group. *I need to use my brain*, he thought. He would try something he hadn't seen done before.

Hoping an immediate change in how he viewed the situation would help him figure out how to catch them, he surfaced for air and spyhopped; he poked his head above the surface and looked around.

He saw land off in the distance. When he turned in a half circle, he also saw land. Then, as he had almost completed a full circle, he saw a multitude of seagulls and cormorants flying just above the water and a few were diving into the water. He knew exactly what was going on, why the birds were acting together with such haste. He echoed and saw precisely what he thought would be there. He dashed for the fish he had convinced himself weren't worth catching. After all, his stomach hurt from hunger, and his fins, tail, and dorsal felt heavy from near exhaustion.

He remembered what his father had told him. *Be aware of everything.*

He fully submerged himself, echoed again, and quickly found the school and dozens of at least six kinds of birds under the water and a hundred or more birds on the surface. Fish crowded near the surface and were less densely packed at the bottom of the shoal.

Had he had more experience, this would have been a warning to him.

He poised at the edge of the chaos, snapped his tail, and rushed into it without locating again. The birds had balled up the herring just as Brian Orca's family would have! *Those birds are brilliant animals*, he thought.

Different kinds of birds working together for a common goal. *They hunted as one, just like us.* He hadn't known birds could do such a thing. Even his parents probably didn't know birds did this. *Wow, a discovery.*

He grabbed a herring near the surface, as big as a young sprinter, then another, even bigger one. He caught a seagull because it was right in front of his mouth. Birds might be amazing, but they were still food. Before he was able to swallow the first gull, he grabbed another. *Yuck.* What a mistake. The seagulls tasted horrible, just awful: he imagined like putrid entrails.

A moment later, he noticed a fast-moving, large shadow whale-like thing closing in on him. Startled, he leaped into the air and breached. As Brian Orca thrust himself into the air, he thought with embarrassment that orcas don't fly out of the water when they feel threatened. But the threat was immediate, so he just reacted. For a moment, it felt as if he had jumped out of his skin—as if his skin was still in the water and his body was in the air.

The instant he was back in the water, he slapped his flukes on the surface, tail lobbing to tell his pod he was in danger. His flukes hit with such power and crispness, the resulting bang echoed in both water and air.

Sudden, terrible pain struck him as if something big had bitten him. *No one can hear me* shot through his mind. *They're too far away!* A lone, fully grown great white shark was a big part of why the fish had massed into the ball and were so densely packed at the surface. They were more afraid of the shark than the birds, even though the birds caught more of them than the shark. When Brian Orca had seen the dark shape, it had circled him, had tasted his scent—his essence in the water—and had thoroughly checked out the situation and was charging him.

Brian Orca was lucky because he had not been bitten. His tail had accidentally hit the shark on the side of her head as she attacked him, knocking her out. She rose slowly to the surface, turning belly up.

Searing pain streaked through Brian Orca's tail as he struck her, and the pain continued as he turned to see the massive upside-down shark.

What's a great white doing in inland waters? Brian Orca thought. Had she followed him?

He hesitated, unsure of what to do. Predatory instinct told him if he swam away and the shark was alive, she would hunt him down. After all, that's what he would do if he were hunting big prey and he had been stunned and then woke up. Brian Orca watched her for any sign of life. She seemed unconscious, and he knew great whites don't do well when belly up because he had watched his parents and other pod and clan adults kill them.

He was alone and in pain. If he didn't act, she would wake up and hunt him. Brian Orca was too much of a prize to let go. The shark was half-again his size, outweighed him, and could quickly kill him. He represented a true feast to her.

Despite the trouble with his tail, Brian Orca attacked. He lunged for the liver as he had seen his parents do and tore into the shark in a frenzy of hunger and, unlike his parents, a bit of fear. After first blood, fear transformed into frenzy and a feast of a lifetime, and he forgot about his tail.

Her liver, oil, and fat reinvigorated him. When his fever was over and his strength fully returned, he gauged how drained he had been. He had been close to exhaustion. *Sometimes one doesn't know what a bad state they're in until they're out of it*, he realized. Of course, he would soon

remember he was also injured.

CHAPTER 3
Kelping

Brian Orca wasn't ordinary. Thanking Wassemo for his feast and saving his life seemed laborious and had little reward. He never got an answer, at least an answer he could perceive when he tried to speak to Wassemo. He had already learned not to take anybody's word at face value, especially if they evoked Wassemo. An orca's observation of cause and effect might be accurate, but he often doubted the given reason behind the cause. Still, he felt guilt. Had Wassemo guided his fins? Did Wassemo somehow tell him to jump out of the water at precisely the right time, and had Wassemo taken control of his tail, fins, and flukes so that he struck the shark at just the right time and in the right place? Did they do all of that and at the same time allow him to be hurt? Or was it only part of Wassemo's doing? But what part? What part of what happened was Wassemo's will, and what part was free will? Were Wassemo responsible for feeding him, for renewing his strength?

Brian Orca felt a tinge of guilt because his family believed Wassemo were the omniscient gods who created everything and determined everything. He now knew for sure he did not believe as his pod believed. To him, the little of the world he had seen was more complicated than his family's beliefs, and as he thought about it, he realized while he didn't believe in certain aspects of Wassemo, he wasn't sure he knew what he believed in.

Brian Orca acknowledged to himself that he Brian Orca, killed the shark. A teenager killed a huge, adult great white that significantly outweighed him. He was able to kill her because of a fortunate accident. If he did see his parents again, and if he did tell them his story of the great white, he was sure they would not believe him. Or they would invoke Wassemo.

His tail throbbed in pain.

He echolocated to get a full read on his surroundings. Fish, a massive kelp forest, a few otters, and several seals were in the vicinity, but nothing significant that could endanger a single, young orca.

He understood immediately the area was a predator's paradise. He echolocated again to ensure there wasn't another big shark in the area and out of new respect for what his parents had taught him. His parents were wrong about Wassemo, but they had been right about always knowing your surroundings. Many of their lessons made sense. But Wassemo, if they ever existed, weren't what this clan said they were. Perhaps Wassemo were made up to impart lessons. If you controlled the narrative of Wassemo, you controlled the pod. Their teachings controlled his family, pod, clan, and community. Yet he knew there were many orcas out there who believed in other creators.

He decided to find out where the seals congregated for future hunting, when he heard a light smack of a pectoral fin against the water's surface. He turned in the sound's direction and sent an echo to get a bead on what was in front of him. The sound came from the kelp. He heard it again. At first, his heart gladdened at the thought it might be his mother or father, but the force of the sound wasn't of tail lobbing or even the pectoral slap of a large orca. It was weak. A dolphin? The sound was too resonant to be caused by the little fin of his distant cousins. Who was it? And why had it not located or greeted him?

His sister? She was teasing him! His heart raced. *Could it be?* But there was no way the little one would dare sneak away from her pod, much less the family.

Brian Orca located in the direction of the slap. He instinctively smacked his tail hard, twice in fact, in quick succession. Sudden, severe pain racked the back of his tail.

Whatever it was, it did not respond. Dread replaced his pain. He should hide. But where? Oh, if only he were with his pod!

But he was an orca, and he was not about to hide. Though hesitant, he echo-located again, and this time saw a lone female orca, about three-quarters of his size, inside the vast forest.

He sounded again and confirmed his observation. Definitely only one orca. Why the response? Her family had to be around.

She has to be a resident, he thought. Despite what he had been taught about avoiding the local pod, he moved toward her, his tail protesting in reawakened pain. *I won't even be able to understand her. Residents sing in gibberish! And they worship The One. In a way, they eat what they worship. They worship a fish that gave, they believe, its life for all orcas.*

Even before his lessons formally started, every adult drilled it into him. Brian Orca's kind must use caution when contacting the resident pods in the different inland seas. The orcas of this inland sea were annoying because they claimed the sprinter for themselves. To avoid conflict, it was agreed by the communities in this part of the Great Blue not to take many sprinters in resident waters. It was an agreement said to have been passed down from Wassemo themselves.

He was supposed to perform a greeting ceremony to be polite and safe if she was a resident. He was not supposed to approach her if she was alone unless he wanted to mate, which meant joining her pod.

Brian Orca surfaced to take a breath. Pieces of shark floated on the surface, and he grabbed the most succulent one. He would make a new greeting ceremony. He would give her a greeting gift, though this decision was not what would make such a difference to orca-kind. He gingerly snapped his tail and spyhopped, causing him much pain. He took time to take a good look around. Nothing was out of the ordinary on the surface, just a lot of birds after scraps of pieces of the shark.

He dove cautiously and headed straight for the female. He located several times as he closed the gap: many fish, but only one orca and no other animal that could threaten him. He was relieved and felt reasonably safe.

The female orca was inside the forest, about an orca's length from the edge of it, and despite the mass of life in front of him, his echo imparted she had kelp draped around the base of her dorsal fin. He thought it was an odd thing residents did; they loved to play with kelp. They would bring it along with them, on their dorsal, pectorals, and even in their mouths sometimes, and they would drop and then retrieve it. Kelping was one of their favorite games.

This orca may have kelp draped over her, but why wasn't she moving around?

As he got closer, he finally received an echo from her, along with a string of singular clicks. Yet she did not whistle. Her language was resident, and her sounds were more staccato, evolved of closed space and not the open ocean.

Her particular tonality and the many singular clicks were not the languages of play in any orca dialect. To him, it seemed to impart loneliness.

She blasted him with varied clicks in multiple bursts intermixed with pulses as he approached. Her loneliness had changed to excitement.

Yet she did not move, neither approaching him nor swimming away.

He reached the edge of the mighty forest. Inside, schools of various-sized fish were interspersed among the massive green blades. The kelp height was more than five times his entire length. It was an amazing place. Near the surface, the forest swayed in rhythmic eddies, and closer-packed schools moved in unison as they kept their relative positions to the massive blades.

He surfaced to grab air and adjusted his grip on the shark meat. He was about to enter the forest from the surface when the shark attack flashed through his mind. So, he dove about a third of the height of the kelp. He moved slowly and found when he put less stress on his tail, he moved with less pain. He wasn't sure what he was getting into; he thought it safer to approach from underneath her. And maybe she wouldn't spook if he approached her slowly.

She echoed toward him. She was not far above, and he heard her slip to the surface to breathe.

He waited at the forest's edge for her to make the next move, flesh in mouth, the kelp in a peaceful cadence above him. At his depth, weak, streaked light barely pierced the multi-layers of blades on narrow stalks above him.

The surface waves, seemingly chaotic when viewed from the air, were rhythmic when experienced from below, and they refracted the light, causing it to flicker and dance about all the life above him.

Silence.

Neither was trying to communicate. *Neither of us is acting orca-like*, he thought. He wondered if he had insulted her by not engaging in a greeting ceremony.

She approached from his side, poking her head from the thick kelp, and then floated upward. She was looking down at him, her body slightly over his.

Startled, he almost dropped the piece of shark. How had she snuck up on him? He turned to her and adjusted his angle. They locked eyes.

The kelp was gone from the base of her dorsal fin. She let go with a sudden burst of clicks, pulsating sounds, and whistles. She was obviously excited. She should be giving chase or taking chase, initiating some movement… something! But she was motionless. She seemed content to eye him while bombarding him with a language he didn't understand. Was she testing him in some way? They should be challenging each other or playing. They should be moving.

He listened and listened as she went on, her fast and excited speech undecipherable.

He finally understood a word. "… really…," then others: "… why… happened."

When he realized he wouldn't understand much more, he interrupted with a whistle. "I don't understand."

She retorted in perfect offshore orca speech. "You really can't, can you?"

"Huh. No." He was confused. "Yes. Yes, I can. I can. Now. You can speak my language?" he blurted out.

"Yes. What in the world do you have in your mouth?" she said. Her tone imparted, taken aback, but he thought she glanced at the meat longingly as she asked.

"Ah, it's, it's shark," he said. "Great white. I killed it myself," he added, with pride.

"Why are you carrying a piece of fish from the open sea?"

"It's for you," he blurted out. Brian Orca was entirely out of his safe zone, and he said the first thing to come to mind. "Is that what you asked me when speaking in your language?"

"For me?" She increased her angle on him a little. "I don't eat shark meat. It's against The One's teachings."

"I know. I know you mostly eat sprinters and other salmon, but it's good, and it's fresh, and I thought you might like it."

"What do you think I am?" She didn't wait for an answer. "What are you doing here? Where is your pod? Are they coming here, too? You're not even a transient!" Her tone and her stiff body became accusatory.

Orcas almost never attack other orcas. Still, maybe she was an exception, he thought. "I got carried away. My pod is not around here."

"Yes, we have already established that. I know that. I do speak your language."

"Of course you do." *Idiot!* he thought. He moved up to her level, and she carefully adjusted her angle so they always directly faced each other.

"Again, what are you doing here?"

"Um, well, I ahh, well, as I said, I got carried away."

"By what, a bird? A whale, maybe? What exactly could carry you here?" There was a bit of sarcasm in her clicks.

"What? No, my family pissed me off so I swam away.

"You left your pod? What a fundamentally stupid thing to do. They didn't follow you, call you back? What did you do? Where are they?"

"I don't know." Brian Orca opened his mouth wide and let his gift slowly rise toward the surface. He felt rejected. "Do you want me to go?" His tail was throbbing again. He supposed it had been throbbing the whole time.

She ascended to the level of the tip of his dorsal by only moving her pectoral fins, looking him over as she did. Brian Orca noticed she was still making sure she faced him head-on. And he saw she controlled her slight ascent in a very un-orca way. She didn't move her tail, moving forward as she ascended. Maybe he could learn from her. His tail hurt a lot less when he kept it still.

So far, he had only seen her head and the front of her pectorals and dorsal. She seemed never to let down her guard. This was one careful orca and maybe one suspicious orca.

"You're hurt," she said.

She surprised him; the suspicious orca was concerned. He twisted his tail to look at it, causing immediate, searing pain. But he refused to let her see his pain. He could not see his injury, but he knew it was where his flukes met his tail.

She clicked and started to look at his injury.

"Don't do that!"

"Are you certain you don't want me to?"

"No! I think it's just sore. I hit the shark a little too hard when I killed it."

"You killed the shark? *You?* Your tail looks like you hit a big rock. I know how it feels. It's starting to bruise. Is a shark's body that hard? Really, you killed the shark? Or did you have help?" She adjusted her position. "You are lying to me. There are no great whites in these waters."

"Well, one attacked me not too far from here. I'm alone. I hit him accidentally," he said quickly and defensively. How stupid he was, he thought, to be hurt by striking a shark with his tail. It was something adults in his pod did all the time… stunning large sharks by hitting them with their tails. *Idiot!*

"Sharks don't attack orcas," she said.

"This one was bigger than me, and I was alone."

He moved his tail and cautiously rose to her level. She had not relaxed and instead watched him carefully, seemingly ready to react should he make the slightest aggressive move.

"I can't explain the great white. Their numbers have increased since the ape's numbers have declined. Maybe it followed me all the way here from where I was when I left my pod. Why do you stay in the kelp? I mean, I know your kind plays in it a lot. You had kelp on you just before I got here. Where is *your* pod?"

She let the current gently push her into green until only her head was visible to him. "You should go away. You need to go back to your pod."

"Do you hear any of my kin? Do you hear any other orca? I'm alone. I have done nothing but say hello and offer you food."

"Go away before I call my family."

"I think you're alone, too."

"Go away."

Very un-orca-like, he thought. He ascended again until he was a pectoral's length above her. She didn't adjust her position this time, and what he saw shocked him. She was emaciated. *How long has it been since she's eaten? She's almost dead!*

He saw her snap on her pectorals to begin an ascent to breathe. *She does everything differently*, he thought. He considered that maybe she'd been adjusting because she had no other choice.

He shot up to the surface, streaking past her in a flash.

He popped his head out of the water. Gulls swarmed pieces of the shark near them, and Brian Orca was immediately annoyed at the pesky things. Without saying a word to her, he swam over to the birds and grabbed the meat, disturbing the gulls. They squawked and shrieked, complaining because their feast was interrupted. He took a breath and dove into the middle of the kelp forest. He echo-located and immediately spotted her. She was maintaining her position just below the surface.

"You're back."

He reached her and nuzzled her mouth with the meat, and she allowed the gesture momentarily. She stared at the meat, and her eyes conveyed temptation.

She rose to the surface and took a deep breath. She tasted the water near the shark. She seemed tempted again. "I'm an outcast," she said matter-of-factly.

"What does that have to do with eating?"

"The rules of The One are many."

"What rule tells you not to eat?"

"It's complicated."

How could her pod allow this? *She seems to be killing herself,* he thought. "Tell me."

"It's faster this way."

He moved slightly to get a better look at her damaged tail. In doing so, he spooked a terrified otter that had been hiding from them, and it darted off.

"I suppose you eat otters, too," she said glumly. "Don't get me wrong; it's not a bad thing you offered me food. I just won't…" She cut herself off.

"I'm Brian Orca," he blurted out.

"Sandy Louise Orca."

"So, if you don't mind me asking, what did you do to deserve this? And why were you alone?"

"It's not about what I deserve." Her gaze wandered off. "Do you believe in a higher power?" she asked.

"What? No. I mean…" He stopped. He didn't want to offend her. And he had no idea what answer would offend her. *What could she know about Wassemo?* he thought. She had to know very little of him.

"I don't believe in The One," she said. "I was the only one in my clan who doesn't."

"It's about belief?"

"No." She hesitated. "Well, yes, sort of. I was kicked out of my pod."

"Kicked out? I've never heard of such a thing. How horrible! Were you kicked out because you didn't believe?"

"No. I left my pod out of curiosity for the world, and when I returned after a month away, they said I had no place among them. I traveled with some of your kin and learned your language. They hate me because I'm different now."

He understood she was no longer one of them because she had taken on the ways of others. She had been gone for an entire month.

"A month." And one of the open water clans let her join them? Then she came back? Wow! *I'm gone from my pod for a few days, and I'm almost killed, and I'm hurt.* His head was full of questions. "Well, I don't believe in your One, either."

"What a surprise," she said in mocking, sardonic clicks. "Though I would ask you why yours is the truth."

"I'm not sure about our One, our Wassemo. I'm not like others in my clan, just like you are not like your clan."

She was silent as she considered what he said.

"I find your Wassemo is very much like our One."

"*Are?*"

"Very demanding—and I'll bet very contradictory as well. It's odd how our all-knowing create us, know everything about everything and are all-powerful, and then they get angry because we don't meet their expectations when they know we won't meet them."

She was right, Brian Orca thought, but he also realized he had an opening and was tired of holding the piece of shark. "Then what's the matter? Eat."

"Brian Orca, I'm not eating because it's faster not to eat."

"Shark won't kill you."

"I didn't say it would."

"I'll catch you something else."

"It's not about the shark meat."

"The One isn't going to hate you!" Brian Orca said.

"Please stop! The truth is, I've eaten sharks before—and octopus and squid. I even grabbed a large mammal once. A cow."

"What?"

"I must pay for my transgressions. I *am* paying for my transgressions. It's simply faster if I don't eat."

Brian couldn't get his mind off Sandy Louise Orca eating a cow. He'd never heard of such a thing! "A cow?"

"After I grabbed the animal, an ape screamed and threw rocks at me, and then it fell over itself. It laughed so hard. It seemed desperate and amused simultaneously, and I got out of those waters quickly."

Brian Orca couldn't help but chitter in laughter. "You are one weird orca."

"I am."

"Please eat."

"Why haven't you left me? Why are you here?"

"Your transgression is you left the pod, learned others' ways, and returned?"

"Pretty much."

Brian Orca searched but had no words because he didn't have an answer, except he was also alone, and she was more like him than any orca in his family, pod, or even his huge clan.

"I must admit, having food right in front of me is difficult. I can taste it."

"Can you? What did you do to deserve death?"

Sandy Louise Orca thrust out her pectoral fins, pushed mightily at the water, and she moved to him. She angled her fins at the last moment to dodge him and grabbed the shark meat from him as she passed. As she glided on, she tore into the flesh with a veracity that would make any orca proud. She made quick work of the meat.

"Is there more? You killed a huge shark."

"You saw me kill it?"

"You both made a lot of noise."

He flicked his tail. "Come on."

She did not move, so he immediately stopped.

"I can't," she said.

"Why? Why won't you trust me?"

She flicked her pectorals, turning her back to him.

Brian Orca approached her, looking her over as he had a slight angle above her. He saw a long, angry-looking gash where the peduncle and caudal peduncle muscles met.

"Wassemo," Brian Orca said. "How?"

Sandy Louise Orca moved her head back and forth. She jutted her head upward. It seemed to Brian Orca that she mimicked the little dolphins when they were nervous or warned each other about something.

"Food?" she said.

"How, Sandy Louise Orca? What did that to you?"

"Stupidity! I was hunting a seal. My clan does not eat seals, but I like them. It was chasing a sprinter, so I thought it would be cool to grab it before the seal could. I went through an archway to cut off the sprinter and slammed against the rock. I must have hit it just right."

She suddenly seemed exhausted to him, as if her meal had given her a boost only to have it jolted from her, leaving her with little energy.

"Why do you deserve death?"

"Because I'm not one of them anymore."

If anything, his pain had gotten worse. But he knew exactly what he had to do. Brian Orca turned, and with everything he had, he dove. He wasn't sure if most of the remaining meat was floating about or had sunk. But he would find it.

He darted through the kelp. He glanced at the kelp blades waving in the currents and the glinting, shimmering light. Focused light formed intense spots so bright it reminded him of the deep-sea light sparkers he had once seen at the bottom of a canyon during the deepest dive of his life.

He started to surface to catch a breath, ensuring some kelp got tangled around his dorsal and pectoral fins. He had kelp on him by the time he broke the surface. He took a deep breath. The kelp draped over his back soothed him a bit, a welcomed momentary distraction. She was going to die. He was sure of it. But she would die with a full stomach. *Wassemo*, he thought, *how could this happen to such an intelligent orca? Wassemo.*

Wassemo? Wassemo, can you heal her? It is said you have such powers! Brian Orca located several large chucks of the shark deep below him. As he dove toward the meat, he made a deal with Wassemo, an agreement with what he was starting to admit was a fantasy. *If you save her, cure her before I return to her, I will believe in you.*

Brian Orca made for the severed tail. In recently learned caution, before he reached it, he echo-located and spotted several orcas who appeared to be converging on the remains of this kill. They veered off when they spotted him, a couple to his left and one to his right. They were exceptionally chatty among each other, firing off a barrage of clicks, whistles, and pulsed calls as they passed him. *What clan are they from?* he wondered.

"Wait!" *Do they know where she is?* he thought. But they did not answer, and they swam off quickly.

CHAPTER 4
Beginning

It was a clear night. Brian Orca and Sandy Louise Orca were at the surface and in the middle of the kelp because both felt safest there, and the kelp calmed the often-choppy surface so she could rest easier. Three weeks had passed since they met. A few members of what he thought were her clan had circled them at a significant distance a few times, only to swim farther off as soon as Brian Orca tried to communicate or approach them. He even tried leaving the immediate area to see if they would rejoin Sandy Louise Orca, but they did not approach her. None offered help. Their standoffishness seemed to outweigh curiosity. He knew Sandy Louise Orca broke the mold for her kind, and Brian Orca knew it because he also broke it. Were they so different? Their kin were going to spurn them permanently?

Brian Orca had fed her multiple times daily at some cost to his health. His bruise had healed entirely and his pain was gone, but he was thinner and not quite as strong as he had been a month ago. In the weeks he had been hunting for two, he had never slimmed down her portion for his benefit. At times he had even stilled his hunger to provide for her. She looked worse; she *was* worse… even more emaciated.

Yet she was still alive.

Her body resulted from little exercise, a weakened immunity system, a festering wound, and a broken bone.

Brian Orca learned her language and dialect. He learned fast, and they could now communicate in two languages.

She rested in the middle of the kelp bed until Brian Orca returned with a giant pacific octopus. The octopus's body was in his mouth, several tentacles hanging between his teeth.

The octopus moved a couple of tentacles, and she grabbed them. Her teeth were serrated, resulting from generations of her clan catching sprinters, relying on them as their preferred food source. The teeth of Brian Orca's pod adults were ground down from killing so many sharks and other large prey. Bones of big prey wore down teeth. Brian Orca's teeth were beginning to wear down, making a slight difference in holding prey with soft, boneless bodies.

"You need to eat. You don't look well, and it's a pain to swim around with a live octopus."

Brian Orca released the large mollusk and backed off a little. Sandy Louise Orca thrust her head to one side; the force of the water jammed the octopus squarely into her mouth.

They rested in silence for a few minutes after her meal, each in their thoughts, Brian Orca fearing he would fail to keep her alive. He would recheck her tail later tonight, he thought.

The wind had died, and the water's surface was still. He spyhopped and looked up and saw thousands of stars. The moon was not out, so the band of the Milky Way stretched across the sky. The purple, orange, and multiple hues of blue were an incredible backdrop draped from horizon to horizon. Many of the stars were bright, like tiny little suns. The adults in his pod believed the lights were part of Wassemo's world, part of where they lived. They were the pure part of the living who had died, and they were now with Wassemo. Brian Orca didn't want to ruin the joy he felt because of the beauty of what he was witnessing, but he was skeptical. Anything attributed to Wassemo was because of Wassemo, and in the back of his mind, that made him feel loss. Wassemo had not answered him. Or they were toying with him.

She poked her head out of the water, but not as far as he did, as she didn't have the strength.

"I think you should leave."

"Not happening."

"You have been taking care of me for too long."

"No," Brian Orca cut her off.

A stillness between them lasted only a moment, but it was a long time for Brian Orca. She followed his gaze, and she, too, looked up at the heavens.

"I wonder what they are. I've always wondered what they are," Sandy Louise Orca said. "We believe they are the spirits of the dead looking down upon us, but I don't know why such a thing would be. Nothing I've experienced suggests anything watches us."

"How did your One create us?"

"The One is unity. It is taught that he created the first orca with a breath and a slap of his mighty tail. It is said he hit the ocean bottom so hard it made the sand at the bottom of the deepest trench swirl into orca shapes, and he then breathed the spark of life into our ancestors. His breath, after all, is the red spark of the flowing, molten rock."

"You've seen the flowing rock?"

"No, I have not."

"I have, deep in the Great Blue. I understand why a clan might call it The One's breath. It heats the water, causing it to bubble, and it creates new land. I don't understand why The One's way means you should die to pay for what you did. I still don't understand why he would want you to die."

She was silent a moment as she mulled over what he said. "Your Wassemo doesn't seem to care. What about him?"

Brian Orca had not told her he had asked Wassemo to save her, and it took him a moment to search for a way to deflect her question. "Them. Wassemo is a quaternity."

"Quaternity?"

"Four. It is taught that all four are equal and are one."

"Just how can one be four and four be one?"

"They are of all the possibilities of who we are, we believe."

"So Wassemo, are not all males?"

"Of course not. They are he, she, they, and the dead. All four is of the one."

"The One is only one."

"Yours is certainly more straightforward," he said. "I always found mine confusing."

"But equally wrong, you're thinking. Yes?"

Brian Orca let out a burst of high pitch clicks to show he was happy with her comment. "We think alike."

"Our clans' ways help us survive, but they don't impart the truth. What they believe is not what is," she said. "Our ways both help and limit us."

True, he thought, *our ways do limit us.* "The One has never spoken to you?"

"No."

"You and I should agree we only accept what is proved to be."

"Yes," she said. "That's it! And accept what is proven not to be!"

The fundamental truth they had found together was momentarily lost on Brian Orca, as his mind had jumped back to Wassemo. Did he deny he believed in everything he had been taught about Wassemo? He still desperately hoped they would save her. He exhaled nervously, shooting water high up into the air.

But then he said it. And when you say something, it seems to make it truer.

"Both Wassemo and The One won't do anything because they can't do anything. Neither exists." It shook him to say out loud what he knew to be true. "Neither exists," he repeated.

Sandy Louise Orca took in a labored breath. She dipped her head under the water, and he immediately followed her.

"You're in bad pain again!" Brian Orca said. He circled to her backside to look at her wound. He sent a series of clicks. He flexed his melon to focus on his sound. He feared knowing the truth, and the thought of losing her made him afraid. But what he saw gave him hope. Underneath her skin and muscle, he saw her fractured bone wasn't as fractured as it had been. He tried to look at her wound to see if it was any better, but without the moon, it was too dark at night to see it in detail.

"It doesn't go away now. But enough of that. I need to ask you a question, and I need you to be truthful, to be honest, to tell me the way it actually is," she said.

He moved close to her. "Of course. Ask me anything you want. Anything."

"What matters is what you think. Not what we hope The One or Wassemo might or might not do. You think I'm going to die soon, don't you?"

What? he thought. *No! No, I won't let you die! But broken bones don't heal!* This was the second time this day he didn't know how to answer her. And he feared it would come to be if he spoke the truth, as if his vocalizing something could make it happen. Perhaps it was better to be in the dark and take it on misplaced faith she might be healed because Wassemo or The One existed and might decide to save her. The belief in someone much more powerful than he could change her fate was comforting. He was confused at the meaning of it all because he wanted her to live and would believe if his belief would save her. Still, it did seem to him only he was trying to keep her alive.

"What did you see?"

"I …" He nudged against her, making soothing contact like a close friend would. "I won't let you die. I will feed you until you get better."

"Why were we created differently than the apes?" she said.

"What? Why would you ask such a thing?"

"The bones of the apes heal," she said. "Ours do not."

"Surely apes' bones don't heal!"

"An ape approached me once. It was in their water skin. It had a healed bone that was once broken. I saw the bone. What if we healed as they do? What if we were made that way, like the apes? I know it's impossible. I'm just wishing…"

"A bone can heal? Are you certain? What did it look like? How do you know?"

"There was this line of denser bone where the break had been. It was like a lightning bolt had struck it and imparted its jagged shape in the bone."

"I have seen lightning. Your bone has the same jagged line, and the gap in the fracture is starting to close in! I think it's starting to heal."

"No."

"I think it is."

"Surely not! But what if it is? So what?"

"So what? I have to keep you alive until your bone heals as your ape's bone did." He moved close to her. "Lightning is awesome," he said in a single set of quiet clicks, cracking a joke. "In the sky or bone."

"You mean the shape of it?"

"Yes."

A moment of silence passed between the two as Sandy Louise Orca collected herself.

"I don't want to die," she said.

Brian Orca whined in slow, evenly pitched clicks. Knowing it would not help her to make promises that seemed too big to keep. He arched his back, flicked his tail, and without another word, left Sandy Louise Orca.

CHAPTER 5
Water Spark

Leaving Sandy Louise Orca was the most difficult thing he had ever done. But he needed to act.

As Brian Orca cleared the forest, he sent out clicks, ticks, and whistles, calling out for his clan, pod, and family. He changed his tonality while announcing he was Brian Orca and was looking for his pod, clan, and community because he knew all of his kin, no matter how far removed, would lead him to his grandmother.

Receiving no answers, he broke into a porpoise, sometimes skimming over the water when he moved in sudden bursts of even greater speed. It was an urgent race for him, slowing to just a porpoise to grab his breath, only to race again as soon as he could. After what was indeed a record time for all orca at such high speeds, he finally had to slow down to a fast swim to avoid exhaustion. He was determined not to stop and keep moving forward until he found his family. He was going to convince them to help him help her.

He swam at the surface for several minutes and was about to dive and swim underwater and to call out again for his family when he tried a pectoral slap. He knew he was far from open water and his pod, but urgency tugged at him. All he had to do was get out of the claustrophobic inland waters. He did not position himself correctly and was swimming, so his slap was pathetic. His plea did not carry far.

He stopped, angled, and slapped the water as hard as possible—this time, his set of loud smacks carried for many miles. The concussive sound reverberated back from opposite directions after it bounced off the land closest to him, to the west and the east. He was heading north. North would eventually take him into the coastal waters of the Great Blue. If his family had left for the deeper open waters, he knew there was little hope of finding them.

The reverberations were quickly followed by crisp returned claps whose origins were close to him. The set was faster than his, and they were as strong as his, but not stronger as if made by a teenager or a young adult like him. Before he could respond, he heard another set and then another. Each was paced differently and from a different direction than the others. He quickly gathered an orca was in front of him, one was to his left, and another was a little farther off to his right.

He echoed several times and saw they were converging on him without any other greeting or announcement they were approaching. Except for the tail slaps, they were silent.

Brian Orca feared they might attack him. What had he done? One orca finally called to him. He recognized its language as that of the residents, but he still could not gauge its intentions because its tonality was neutral.

Why were they closing in on him, triangulating as if they were hunting?

They began to circle him like his pod would hunt a big adult shark. Brian Orca had no idea what to do. He considered fleeing. He had once witnessed a clan attack one of their own. Such attacks happen once or twice a generation and are always uniquely warranted. And it was brutal and bloody and final. It was said residents never attacked their own—such little comfort.

He slipped under the water, settling a body's length from the surface. He wasn't a dumb shark. He wouldn't let them get under him.

A female about his age was the first to break the circle to swim to him. She stopped several body lengths in front of him. Curiously, she positioned herself at the surface.

Upon arrival, the second orca swam to the first's left. He stayed at the surface as well.

The third arrived seconds after, and she playfully forced her way between the two, purposely nosing at and bumping into the other two.

Brian Orca's heart skipped a couple of beats in relief. Sensing safety and even celebration, he quickly surfaced.

The four burst out in long, modulating whistles, long calls, and joyful clicks. The three made for him, and he for them. They met, and the four swam around each other, then with each other in unison, nosing and touching. Brian Orca already so missed the play and the pure joy being with many other orcas brought. He did not know the three, yet they enjoyed a greeting ceremony, which soon became a joyful ruckus.

But the ruckus was short-lived, and they had not even given each other their names when one of the females who seemed to like to play stopped the celebration with a quick burst of sequential clicks.

Brian Orca gauged them. They all seemed to be around his age, and the largest of them, a male with a big scar from a gash in his dorsal fin, was half a jaw longer than Brian Orca. His dorsal fin was long and becoming prominent, so Brian Orca guessed the male was probably three or so years older. Both females seemed odd to him. Both spoke in a dialect, a language he didn't recognize, and neither had the super sharp teeth the male or Sandy Louise Orca had.

"My name is Emica Aoi Orca."

"I am Bo Gang Orca," said the male.

"I am called Lesedi Orca," said the other female.

"And I am—"

"Brian Orca!" Lesedi Orca said.

Brian Orca was astonished. "What? How do you know my name?"

"We have been listening and watching," Lesedi Orca said.

"They were you? All of you? Are there more of you?"

"Unfortunately, no," Emica Aoi Orca said.

"We are worried, Brian Orca," Lesedi Orca said.

"You use two names, not three." *Like my pod*, he thought, *but you're not of my pod or community.*

"Some, in the southern seas, use only one," Bo Gang Orca said.

"And others use up to seven," Emica Aoi Orca said with a twirl of laughing clicks. "We met a Tsnom George Inaki Tobias Won Hume Orca far south of the middle of the Great Blue one season ago. He was my age and hunted seal on the beach."

"She liked him," Lesedi Orca said.

"You all have traveled that far?"

Emica Aoi Orca moved closer to Brian Orca. Her demeanor changed from warmth and easygoing to seriousness. "After watching you, seeing how you have sacrificed and have become such good friends with Bo Gang Orca's sister, we have decided to ask you why you were helping her."

"Why are you leaving her is the more important question," Bo Gang Orca said.

"So it is," Emica Aoi said.

"Sister?"

"Why yes," Bo Gang Orca said.

"We know she has a broken bone and is dying. You helped her, and now you left her," Emica Aoi Orca said. "Why did you stay for so long?"

"Why are you leaving her?" Bo Gang Orca said.

"I'm going to the open waters to find my family."

"Why?" Lesedi Orca said. She circled him, looking him over. "We know there is no hope for her."

"No!" Brian Orca said.

"We wanted to help," Bo Gang Orca said.

"But you haven't!"

"How do you help an orca with a broken bone? A broken bone means death," Lesedi Orca said.

"Yet she has not died." Bo Gang Orca shuddered.

"And she won't! You can help her. You can feed her."

"Why are you returning to your family?" Lesedi Orca said. "We can all feed her together, including you."

"She needs more than food. Her tail is healing, but something else is wrong with her, and I don't know what it is. She has a sickness in her, and it is getting worse, and I only know of one orca who might be able to help."

"Healing?" Bo Gang Orca said.

"You are not leaving it up to your divine spirit to determine her fate? You intend to come back to her?" Lesedi Orca said. "Are you not feeding her and giving credit to your Wassemo?"

Brian Orca's heart sank. Could he tell them what he believed? Would they be willing to feed Sandy Louise Orca if they knew what he did not believe?

"Surely you are leaving because you trust in your Wassemo?" Lesedi Orca said.

"Yes. You are leaving her fate to Wassemo," Bo Gang Orca said.

"No! I will put my trust in you. You feed her while I am gone."

"We are like you," Emica Aoi Orca said warmly.

"What do you mean, like me?"

"We are free of our clans," Bo Gang Orca said.

"Yes, free," Lesedi Orca added.

"And—and I speak for us all—you have helped us see we might be able to help heal a bone," Emica Aoi Orca said. She happily started to swim around him in a tight circle.

He wanted to tell them, to admit he did not depend upon any deity. "I helped her because all we had at the moment was each other, and I don't want her to die." He hesitated to say anything more. But all three waited for him. "I don't believe our truths are accurate."

"You don't believe in your Wassemo?" Bo Gang Orca asked. "Or in The One?"

"We don't either," Lesedi Orca said.

"We believe in ourselves and other orcas," Emica Aoi Orca said. "And in play!" She charged him, then broke off at the last moment.

"Wait. What?" Brian Orca said.

"We are outcasts," Emica Aoi Orca said.

"You don't believe?"

"We are like you," Emica Aoi Orca said.

Brian Orca was amazed to find still others who thought as he did. But Sandy Louise Orca needed his help now. "I have to find my clan."

"The one you say can help is of your clan?" Bo Gang Orca sounded hopeful.

"She, or maybe he, would have to be," Lesedi Orca said. "Who else does he know?"

"Feed her. Keep her alive until I get back?"

"We will," Bo Gang Orca said with resolution. "We will help my sister."

"We will help you do something that has never been done before," Emica Aoi Orca said.

"We will help you heal a bone," Lesedi Orca said.

Lesedi Orca nudged Bo Gang Orca, and he nuzzled her back.

"Oh, they're not together," Emica Aoi Orca said. "He left his pod some time back. He left his sister alone and feels responsible because he was not there to protect and guide her. He's wrong."

Nothing but hope was in Bo Gang Orca's eyes.

Brian Orca turned to Bo Gang Orca. "Help her."

Brian Orca did not wait for a response.

CHAPTER 6
Spark

He was swimming quickly, thinking of the three. He was unsure if they would help Sandy Louise Orca, and he was glum from thoughts that no orca could help. What if he didn't find his pod? Realization of the inevitable, realization Sandy Louise Orca's fate might indeed be Wassemo's to determine, irked him. He had no idea what her brother would do, though he was hopeful he could help her by just being with her. He hoped her brother's presence might lift her spirits and give her strength.

On the thought of Sandy Louise Orca and her brother reuniting, Brian Orca's sister crossed his mind, and he instantly missed her fiercely. Did she miss him as much as he missed her?

He was scanning, constantly echoing now. He wanted to be vigilant, and he didn't want to be surprised again.

It had not been long since he had left the three when he spotted another orca heading toward him. This one was large and swimming fast. *Another outcast?* He quickly recognized the orca's profile by the pure grace of how she swam and the steady way she moved. It was his matriarch… his grandmother. She was alone, and she was racing toward him.

By Wassemo, what is wrong? He thought. *What happened?* Why was she here, so far from her pod?

He was joyous he had found her, or rather, she had found him.

He porpoised, fast and direct.

His grandmother broke out in joyful song. She whirled around him, fully breached, arched her back, and dove into the water. He began to circle her, too. He also breached and slapped at the water and sang in a joyful reunion.

After several minutes of noisy celebration, his grandmother stopped dead in the water and faced him. "What in the world were you thinking?"

She was always to the point, and he had no idea how to answer her.

"Grandma, I'm sorry!"

"You know what I've told you about that word."

"I know; an orca is never sorry. We are not sorry animals. I apologize."

"For what?" She ticked off a quick whistle. She was happy and had been teasing Brian Orca.

Brian Orca swam to his grandmother. They brushed against each other in their familial greeting.

"Where's the pod? Where's my sister? My mom and dad? They're mad at me, right?" He had many questions and had to ask them before he could reveal the real reason he was headed back. Then it dawned on him. "Why are you alone?"

"They're on the other side of the big island about a day north."

"You've been in these waters the whole time I was gone?"

"We're in these waters to look for you. But we'll talk about that later."

He recognized the bait, but he was too worried about taking it. "I have to ask a great favor of you, grandmother."

"I know what you have been doing, Brian Orca. You were already the talk of many pods when we got here."

"What?"

"Child, I know many orcas. She won't survive."

"Don't say that. How do you know? What if I told you she might? With your help, she might. But only you can help her."

"Me?"

"Her bone is healing. But she is sick. If we can make her less sick, her bone will heal more, and she will live." He added, "I hope."

"Hope? One of the main pillars of Wassemo."

"I know. Hunt, hope, faith, love."

"Yes."

"But I was not speaking of it in the way you speak of it, though I suppose my feeding her has been an act of hope, at least in a way."

"In the ways of Wassemo."

"Grandma, I am not asking for Wassemo's help. I am asking for *your* help."

"If I can help, you would be receiving help through them. Such is the way. They act through us."

Brian Orca's emotions were draining away. He was confused by her sudden lecture and her observation on faith about faith. He thought on it momentarily, realizing that debating her was pointless.

"You can only say that if you try to help her. They can't act through you if you don't help me."

"The question, young one, is how can I help? Healing is for Wassemo," she countered.

"Seaweed."

"Seaweed?"

"You told me it can heal."

"Did I?"

"You said it is good for your stomach and healing."

"It's not like I eat it all the time. And I don't even know if the seaweed will help. Stomach pains are no broken bone."

"The bone is healing. She is ill from something other than the bone."

"The seaweed might have been how Wassemo helped heal a cut a few years back. Maybe," she said thoughtfully.

"So, you were exaggerating."

"My generation does that." She added, "It healed faster than normal. We were in a time of less prey before the apes' decline, and Wessemo took pity on me so I could help our pod through lean years."

"Will you help me? There are many kinds of seaweed. Will you show me what kind you eat?"

"Hope in you is strong."

"It is." Brian Orca was on the verge of anger. If she countered one more time, he knew he would say things he would regret for a long time. His grandmother thought in circles and wasn't listening to him! "I ask you not because of faith but hope… in the seaweed."

"Wassemo's seaweed."

"Fine," he said tersely. He had never spoken to his grandmother in such a way, never felt toward her in such a way. "Yes. Yes, Wassemo's seaweed."

"I will show you."

"Thank you."

"You will come back when Wassemo shows their course?"

"What do you mean?"

"Whatever happens to her, you will return to us, Wassemo willing. We miss you."

Brian Orca stared at her for a moment because he was in shock. She would not give up Wassemo for a moment. Yet he was happy to hear his family all missed him.

"I will," he managed to say. But he thought he would not. No matter his condition, he had no intention of eventually seeking redemption from his pod, Wassemo, or his grandmother. He was never going to say he was sorry for leaving.

Brian Orca's grandmother angled downward toward the shallow seafloor. "Follow me."

Only to the seaweed, he thought. *I will not otherwise follow you anymore.*

His grandmother led them along the flat, sandy, yet muddy seabed toward the shore. They traveled over a vast colony of sea pens, all inflated with seawater, all looking like bloated orange feathers. Soon the colony became less dense, and various types of starfish, sea cucumbers, and giant chitons were interspersed among the colony. They passed jellyfish, a couple of octopuses, a huge old rockfish, and seals.

As they neared a big kelp forest, they swam into a couple of schools of young salmon and over scores and scores of sea urchins. *So much food,* he thought. But it was a fleeting thought, as his mind was on Sandy Louise Orca's battle for her life.

The matriarch led him around the kelp forest and into the water, where his belly skimmed the soft bottom, and his dorsal was above the waves. She stopped in front of a large group of boulders.

She tore at a milky greenish-white seaweed attached to the rocks; with a bunch of it in her mouth, she turned to him with difficulty as she was bigger than he, and the water depth was more constrictive for her. She dropped it when they were out of the shallows for him to grab.

"This is the seaweed."

He grabbed as much as he could and nodded in thanks to her. He was about to turn around to rush away to Sandy Louise Orca when his grandmother blocked his way.

"You are going to try to carry the seaweed to her? You'll need to find some near her."

"It will save time if I can." Brian Orca swam to her and gently touched her side in thanks as he passed her.

She let him go. "Goodbye."

Brian Orca swam off.

It took Brian Orca hours to reach Sandy Louise Orca and the others. To his surprise, Bo Gang Orca, Emica Aoi Orca, and Lesedi Orca were tending to Sandy Louise Orca.

He still had the seaweed in his mouth.

Oh no. Sandy Louise Orca was not doing well. She was in the middle of the forest and was at the surface. Her breathing was labored, and her eyes were half shut. Her slow, sporadic ticks and a weak squeal as she talked to her brother told of a significant loss of strength.

Yet Brian Orca noticed her tone, and bearing had a quiet, inner peace. He immediately suspected her peace resulted from the presence of her brother. He was at her side. Emica Aoi Orca and Lesedi Orca were swimming a little erratically around them, like nervous dolphins around a wounded calf. Bo Gang Orca was the quiet presence who helped Sandy Louise Orca be at peace.

"He's back!" said Emica Aoi Orca.

"Yes!" said Lesedi Orca. "Just in time."

"Shhh!" Emica Aoi Orca said to Lesedi Orca. "Where is her help?" she said to Brian Orca.

"She's gotten—"

Bo Gang Orca cut Emica Aoi Orca off with a single, sharp whistle.

Is she that bad? Brian Orca thought as he passed Emica Aoi Orca, then Lesedi Orca.

"Hello to both of you," he said.

"Hello." Emica Aoi Orca was not her usual joyful self.

"We should talk," Lesedi Orca said. Then she noticed seaweed in his mouth. "What in the oceans are you doing with seaweed in your mouth?"

Both turned to follow him as he reached Bo Gang Orca.

"I'm glad you're here, Brian Orca." Bo Gang Orca's eyes showed sadness. He then turned to cut off Lesedi Orca as she was about to add to her observation. "Not now, not here."

Lesedi Orca stopped. She wavered, rocking nervously back and forth. Emica Aoi Orca swam around her friend, touching her to reassure her.

Brian Orca reached Sandy Louise Orca. She tipped her head up to look at him. She noticed the seaweed in his mouth and managed a smile.

"Where have you been?"

"Oh, here and there. I found you healing food."

She laughed in quick bursts of ticks and clicks. "Seaweed?"

"Seaweed."

"Seaweed is not food, even for you, who eats everything."

With effort, she turned to expose her wound to him. "Aren't you supposed to put it on my tail?" She ticked in soft yet hopeful laughter.

Brian Orca saw her tail was inflamed, and her wound looked raw and angry.

"You don't want me to eat seaweed, do you?"

Her wound was festered with a couple of open, deep sores. *She has to be in agonizing pain*, he thought. She was so strong, so brave! She was an inspiration to him… how she held herself together!

"I still don't believe in The One," she said. "I have been helped only by all of you."

"I could believe in Wassemo if it meant you would live," Brian Orca said. His heart was broken, and his mood was dire. Nothing could help her. He felt panic.

The other three orcas swam up to them.

"Indeed, The One has not helped her," Sandy Louise Orca's brother said. "Or your Wassemo."

"I have concluded since all living things are born atheists, and we here are all now atheists, no grand other will help. Only we can help us," Lesedi Orca said.

"Worst of all ways," Emica Aoi Orca joked. "We're on our own," she added.

"Perhaps not quite true. Other orcas know more about certain things than we do. I believe we have already been helped," Brian Orca said. He didn't know what to do next, so he, maybe a little too playfully, placed a bit of seaweed on her wound. He knew it might cause pain, but he did it to lighten the moment. As he put it on her, he immediately thought he had made a mistake while waiting for her to screech in protest.

But she didn't react. It was as if her wound was so nasty that she felt no pain.

"Thank goodness. Better there than in my mouth. I don't want to eat the stuff," Sandy Louise Orca said.

"Why would he want her to eat seaweed, and why place it on her tail?" Emica Aoi Orca said to Lesedi Orca.

"My matriarch," Brian Orca said in low clicks. "She said it is good for healing."

The three orcas looked at each other. Brian Orca knew that the opinions and doings of a matriarch of any pod anywhere carried great weight, and their expressions told him his new friends felt no different.

Bo Gang Orca looked at his sister with worry in his dark eyes. He moved to Brian Orca and grabbed a piece of seaweed. He then angled to face his sister. He chomped on the seaweed. Bo Gang Orca could not entirely hide his sudden disgust. "You'll have to get used to it." He forced himself to swallow it. He nudged his sister with his snout. "Your turn."

"Eat it," Lesedi Orca chimed in.

"Yes. Brian Orca's matriarch says it is good for you," Emica Aoi Orca said with light sarcasm.

"She eats it when she's feeling sick. And she's not just my pod's matriarch; she is my grandmother."

"Wait, what?" Lesedi Orca said. "Your matriarch actually really eats seaweed?"

"We are all here for you," Bo Gang Orca said.

Brian Orca inched closer to Sandy Louise Orca, offering her the seaweed.

"My last meal is to be of seaweed?" she asked sardonically as she took it. But there was trust in her eyes. She chomped down on the macroalgae, and she ate it.

Seven days and seven nights passed. The first three days and nights, the four helped the one, and it was exhausting for all as Sandy Louise Orca sometimes could not even stay afloat to breathe; she was so weak. They fed her all kinds of food from the sea, and twice a day they fed her the white seaweed and kept her wound covered with it.

On the fourth day, she gained enough strength to breathe and move a little on her own.

On the seventh day, seeing her wound was healing, she had gained strength and was her old, sometimes sarcastic self; Brian Orca started to swim off. Sandy Louise Orca followed; then, the others followed one by one. Brian Orca led them away from the forest and toward the open sea. He was not destined to be their leader, as he was destined to seek out others in faraway waters. But that is another story.

They had a pod of their own. They were determined to learn and not accept limitations brought about by the lore and the fallacies of the past. In time, their pod grew into a vast community. Eventually, they would explore the heavens and visit the lights in the night sky, and their discoveries and accomplishments would surpass those of the apes'. But on this day, on the seventh day of their decision to go out on their own and bring others a new way of thinking, a mark in time was checked on a 4.5-billion-year-old planet. It marked the spark of the first civilization created by those of the

sea.

About the Author

Author, screenwriter, and tech-writer Bill Hoffman has a Master of Professional Writing degree from USC. While working in film and television, he sold/optioned several scripts and was a producer. He's also held minor elected office. More importantly, he's been a certified PADI diver since 1977 and, in two oceans, has quite accidentally found himself close and personal among orcas in the wild. Bill lives in WA State.